Matt's Mitt
&
Fleet-Footed Florence

Also by Marilyn Sachs

MARILYN SACHS

Matt's Mitt
&
Fleet-Footed Florence

illustrated by Charles Robinson

E. P. DUTTON   NEW YORK

Matt's Mitt was first published in 1975 by Doubleday & Company, Inc., with illustrations by Hilary Knight. *Fleet-Footed Florence* was first published in 1981 by Doubleday & Company, Inc., with different illustrations by Charles Robinson.

Library of Congress Cataloging-in-Publication Data

Sachs, Marilyn.
   Matt's mitt; &, Fleet-footed Florence.

   Summary: In the first of these two baseball stories, the mitt given at Matt's birth by his errant uncle possesses unusual qualities which shape his life. In the sequel, the fleet-footed star of the North Dakota Beavers meets her match when she encounters Yankee catcher, Fabulous Frankie.
   1. Baseball stories, American.   2. Children's stories, American.   [1. Baseball—Fiction.   2. Short stories]
I. Sachs, Marilyn. Fleet-footed Florence. 1989.
II. Title.   III. Title: Matt's mitt.   IV. Title: Fleet-footed Florence.
PZ7.S1187Matb   1989   [Fic]   88-30980
ISBN 0-525-44450-5

Published in the United States by E. P. Dutton, a division of Penguin Books USA Inc.

Published simultaneously in Canada by Fitzhenry & Whiteside Limited, Toronto

Editor: Ann Durell

Printed in the U.S.A.   First Edition
10 9 8 7 6 5 4 3 2 1

for baseball nuts everywhere,
and especially for my son, Paul

Matt's Mitt

When Matt was born, his parents were very happy. They gave him a party and invited only the best people in the family.

There was his Aunt Louise who came. She was a librarian, and she brought him the *Universe Encyclopedia* as a gift. It had many volumes.

His Uncle Roger, who was an aeronautical engineer, came too. He brought a model of the Wichita Falls Airport, complete with hangars, control towers, airport personnel, airplanes, and one ambulance with flashing lights.

His twin cousins, Bernard and Benedict, were both invited. They were bankers, and they brought a toy bank that was also a music box. If you put a dime in it, a piano played "My Country 'tis of

Thee." If you put a quarter in it, two violins and two cellos played the "Star-Spangled Banner," and if you put in fifty cents, a complete orchestra played the first movement of Beethoven's Fifth Symphony. Nothing happened if you put in a penny or a nickel.

There were other important members of the family who came. They gave beautiful and useful presents. Some of them gave cash.

Matt's Uncle William Edgar was not invited, but he came anyway. Matt's Uncle William Edgar was not an important member of the family. He did not work, and he spent all of his time enjoying himself.

He brought a gift too. It was a baseball mitt. It was blue, and it wasn't new. Matt's mother said thank you because she had good manners. She thought she would throw the mitt away when the party was over and Matt's Uncle William Edgar had gone home.

But she forgot to throw it away. Instead, the mitt was accidentally gathered up with some of the useful and beautiful gifts and put up in the attic until Matt was old enough to appreciate them.

When Matt was seven, he found the mitt. Even though it was large, it fit him perfectly. He kept it with him all the time and slept with it at night.

His mother tried to throw it away while he was sleeping. But Matt's mitt appeared to him in a dream and woke him up in time.

His father offered him a brand-new, expensive mitt with reinforced air holes and natural rawhide lacing, but Matt said no.

When he started to play baseball, Matt could hit very well—as well as other boys. He could run very well—as well as other boys. And he could catch very well. Very, *very* well. Much better than other boys.

Sometimes a boy on his team would ask to borrow Matt's mitt. But the mitt didn't fit on anybody else's hand. Only on Matt's hand. On either hand.

Matt grew bigger and bigger. The mitt stayed the same. But it always fit him.

He was discovered by three baseball scouts when he was seventeen—on the same day.

One asked him to go west and play for the Oakland A's.

One asked him to go east and play for the New York Mets.

And one asked him to go south and play for the Houston Astros.

But he really wanted to go north and play on the new team that had just been formed—the North Dakota Beavers.

So he said no to the three scouts. The next day he was discovered by a scout from the North Dakota Beavers, and he said yes.

Everybody knows what happened after that. Everybody knows how the North Dakota Beavers grew up in ten years from a boondoggle team, made up of raw rookies who lost nine games out of ten, to the World Series champions of twelve straight years in a row.

Some say it was because of expert coaching.

Some say it was because of Lefty Katz, the great pitcher.

Others point out how Spike Gomez stole more bases in one year than any two other players together. And some will tell you that Rick Dooley's batting average never fell below .361 in all the years he played for the Beavers.

But most people know it was Matt—and his mitt.

Matt played center field. He could catch jumping—running—standing—crawling—sitting—lying—turning — twisting — backhand — fronthand — over-hand—underhand—and either hand.

He caught balls that the left fielder missed and balls that the right fielder missed.

And he never dropped a ball. Not once!

But one day he dropped his mitt on Cookie Rogers's head after Cookie referred to his mitt as a "mutt." The umpire broke it up and threw both of them out of the game for the day.

The umpire's name was Ruth (Babe) Jackson, the first woman umpire in the major leagues. Later, she and Matt got married. She didn't mind that he kept his mitt with him all the time.

One day, a jealous outfielder from a rival team stole Matt's mitt and tried to use it himself. He dyed the mitt brown, but it squeezed his fingers and he could not catch.

Even though it was brown, Matt knew it was his own mitt and rescued it. The jealous outfielder said he only did it for a laugh. But nobody laughed. Not even his own teammates.

Matt scrubbed and scrubbed until he got all the dye off, and his mitt looked like its old blue self again.

The time came when Matt was ready to retire. Matt's mitt was ready to retire too. Its seams were splitting, its blue color was fading to gray, and there were deep wrinkles everywhere.

The last day came. It was in the World Series that the North Dakota Beavers played against the New York Yankees. The score was tied, three games to three. Today would wind it up.

In the bottom of the ninth inning, the score was 2–2, with the Yankees up. The first man walked. The second man doubled.

A man on third and a man on second! And no outs. It looked bad. The manager and the catcher went out to talk to the pitcher. He hung his head. It was all over for the pitcher.

A new pitcher came out to the mound. He chewed his gum on the right side of his mouth and threw a curveball with his left hand. The batter swung. Strike one!

The pitcher shifted his gum to the left side of his mouth and threw a sinker with his left hand. The batter did not swing. Strike two!

The pitcher moved his gum back to the right side of his mouth and threw a knuckleball with his left hand. The batter swung.

It looked like a home run. Up, up, up, the ball soared. Above the pitcher's head. Up, up, up. Above the shortstop's head. Up, up, way up, and there were tears in Matt's eyes. He did not want to see his team, the North Dakota Beavers, go down to defeat on his last day.

So he ran back, way back, against the center field wall, and he jumped high and higher and still higher. He was right up under the ball, but it was way above his head. He stretched up his arm as high as it could go, and Beaver fans moaned and screamed because they knew he could not reach it.

They saw the ball zipping its way out over the back wall.

Some say this never happened!

And some say the sun was too bright that day to say for sure what really happened.

But there are those who swear that when Matt could not leap up high enough to reach the ball, Matt's mitt left his hand and made the catch by itself.

When Matt's feet touched the ground again, the mitt was back on his hand, and in the mitt was the ball.

There was silence in the stadium. Even though Matt had caught the ball (or had he?) the runner was advancing from third base on his way home. If only one run scored, the game would be over and the Beavers would lose.

From 461 feet away, Matt could see home plate open and shining in the sun. Nobody had ever thrown a ball so far before. Matt was tired. His arm ached from all that stretching. He took a deep breath. His mitt tightened itself around the ball. He threw, and the ball flew fast, and faster, back

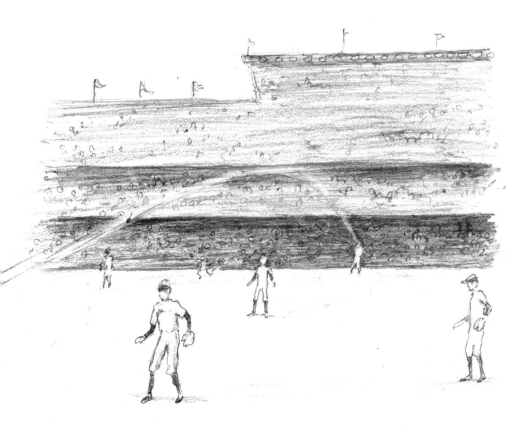

over the head of the shortstop, over the head of the
pitcher, right smack into the catcher's mitt in plenty
of time for the second out, and a throw to third for
the third out.

The ballpark exploded. It was a triple play. And
Matt was the hero.

The Beavers won the series in the tenth inning.

Later, there were parades, parties, speeches, and
medals.

Mostly for Matt.

17

Five years later, Matt was elected to the Baseball Hall of Fame, and his mitt was placed in a glass case right next to Babe Ruth's uniform.

But the mitt wasn't happy.

And Matt wasn't happy.

They missed each other.

So today if you go to the Baseball Hall of Fame
in Cooperstown, New York, you should look carefully at the guides who show people around. One
of them is a skinny little fellow with a big smile.

Watch him carefully. He will tell you everything
you want to know about Willie Mays's baseball and
Joe DiMaggio's bat. He will stop before each of the
famous trophies of great players and tell you facts
you never knew.

But see how he passes by the glass case containing a faded blue wrinkled mitt with bursting seams. He does not look at it, and he does not pause or tell you anything about it. The other guides do, but not this one.

But come back in the evening, after the museum has closed and everybody has gone home. Look through the window and watch as the skinny little fellow with the big smile comes back down the hall. Now he stops in front of the case. He unlocks it. He reaches inside, and when he turns around you will see that the faded old blue mitt is on his hand.

Now you know that Matt and his mitt are together again, enjoying the quiet of the evening, hand in hand.

Fleet-Footed Florence

Matt, the famous baseball hero, had three sons. He hoped that they would become baseball players too.

The first one was named Willie M., after the great hitter. But the only thing Willie M. was great at hitting was his younger brother.

The second one was named Lou B., after the great base stealer. But Lou B. was only great at stealing cookies from the cookie jar.

The third one was named Johnny B., after the great catcher. But the only thing Johnny B. ever caught was colds.

Matt had a daughter too. He didn't expect *her* to become a baseball player, so he named her Florence N., after the great nurse.

One day, there was a fire a few blocks away from where Matt lived. Matt stood on the porch and watched. First, he saw the fire engines go by. Then he saw the police car go by. Then he watched the neighborhood kids run by. He saw Willie M. and Lou B. and Johnny B. then he saw a blue whoosh.

"What," he asked a neighbor, "was that blue whoosh?"

"That blue whoosh," replied the neighbor, "was your daughter, Florence."

Then Matt knew that his daughter, Florence N., would grow up to be a baseball player.

Matt taught her how to hit. And he taught her how to catch. He taught her how to throw. But he did not have to teach her how to run.

When Florence N. grew up, she went to play on her father's old team, the North Dakota Beavers. They had won thirteen World Series in a row in the days Matt played for them. But ever since he left, they had been in a slump.

Florence changed all that. She was the fastest runner in the West. And the fastest runner in the East. The fastest runner in the North. And the fastest runner in the South.

Nobody ever ran as fast as Florence. When she came up to bat, everybody on the opposing team trembled. Because they knew that once she got on base, if there was nobody in front of her, she would come home.

Her fans called her Fleet-Footed Florence, and every game you could hear them shout, *"Hooray for Fleet-Footed Florence!"*

But her enemies called her Flat-Footed Florence or Fatheaded Florence, and often both. Every game, you could hear them shout, *"Phooey on you, Fatheaded, Flat-Footed Florence!"*

27

Florence played center field. She could run faster than the ball. So when she caught it, if there was a runner trying to advance after the catch, she generally ran in to tag him out.

She specialized in four outs. Whenever the bases were loaded, and she caught a fly ball, she liked to run in and personally tag each player out as he returned to his base.

Sometimes her enemies called, *"Break a leg, Flat-Footed Florence!"*

She did once, tripping over a beer can flung on the field. But she played anyway. And stole two bases instead of three, and put only three men out instead of four.

She could hop faster than most people could run. Sometimes when her team was leading, she would play with one leg tied behind her back.

The North Dakota Beavers won the pennant the first year Florence came to play on their team. And that year, they faced their old enemies, the New York Yankees, in the World Series.

Now, the mightiest Yankee of all was Fabulous Frankie, the magnificent catcher. Frankie could catch, and Frankie could hit, and Frankie could throw.

But Frankie could not run as fast as Florence. And Frankie had a habit of hitting balls out toward center field. Which meant that Florence made more four-outers off Frankie's fly balls than off anybody else's.

This made Frankie angry—very angry, very, *very* angry. So angry, in fact, that he flipped. Every time Florence caught his fly balls or tagged out his team-mates, or stole three bases under his nose, he flipped. He flipped so much that he became known as Frankie, the Yankee Flipper.

The worst thing was that he lost his cool. He lost his appetite too, and he lost his sleep. He started letting pitches get by him, and North Dakota Beaver fans began yelling, *"Fumble-Fingered Frankie, the Yankee Flipper! Yaa! Yaa! Yaa!"*

Nobody called him Fabulous anymore.

One day, after the Beavers had won their third
World Series game off the Yankees, and were trying
for their fourth, Florence hit a tiny, baby bunt, and
came flying around the bases into home plate just as
Frankie was picking it up.

They met head on. Eyeball to eyeball. It was the
first time they had ever been so close to one
another.

After that, Frankie didn't seem to mind when
Florence made four outs off his fly balls. And
sometimes, Florence even counted to ten before she
ran in and made her four outs.

It was in all the papers: FLEET-FOOTED FLORENCE
FLIPS OVER FABULOUS FRANKIE.

Soon after, they got married.

Frankie was traded to the North Dakota Beavers, and he and Florence became the most famous pair of lovers in baseball history. They did live happily ever after, too, but that is not the end of the story.

Florence set so many records that there was no book big enough to hold them all. Most great baseball players become famous because of their RBI's* or ERA's** or just their BA's.*** Florence, alone, is also famous for being the only player to have an outstanding record of RCI's.****

Of course she had to make sure that each player she carried in touched each base before she did.

One day, an old woman, dressed in a shabby base-ball cap and jacket, stood outside the dugout asking for autographs. All the other players hurried by, except for Florence.

She smiled at the old woman. She inquired after her health. And she autographed her scorecard. "Fleet-Footed Florence," said the old woman, "you are the greatest baseball star who ever lived."

---

* Runs Batted In
** Earned Run Average
*** Batting Average
**** Runs Carried In

"Ah," sighed Florence, "I wish I might always be a star."

The old woman drew out from under her warm-up jacket a golden baseball. "Because you are good and kind as well as a great star, I have it in my power to grant you your wish."

Then the old women threw the ball with all her
might, and Florence said, "Never fear, ma'am, I will
retrieve that ball for you."

So saying, she hurried after the glittering ball.
Faster and faster it rolled, and faster and faster
Florence ran after it. Out of the stadium, through
the parking lot, and over the city streets spun the
golden ball. Right behind it came Florence, laugh-
ing in the joy of the race. And right behind Florence
came Frankie, crying, "Florence, wait for me!"

Suddenly, the ball rose up into the sky, and Florence reached back for Frankie, and leaped.

Florence was never seen again. Neither was Frankie. Some say they are raising a family of future ballplayers—five girls and four boys.

Some say they are traveling incognito, and can be seen scouting every sandlot where future ballplayers are most likely to be found. Maybe so.

But I think you should look carefully up at the sky on a clear night. Do you really think that flashing, glittering light that moves faster than anything else up there is only a shooting star? Watch! Here it comes again, and see, it really is not a shooting star. You know who it really is racing across the heavens, carrying Frankie in her arms, flying faster than the moon, faster than the sun, faster than any of the other stars.

Fleet-Footed Florence, for all time now, the fastest
star in the firmament.